MARGRET & H.A. REY'S

Curious George

Goes to a Chocolate Factory

Illustrated in the style of H. A. Rey by Vipah Interactive

Houghton Mifflin Company   Boston

Based on the character of Curious George®, created by Margret and H. A. Rey.
Illustrated by Vipah Interactive: C. Becker, D. Fakkel, M. Jensen, S. SanGiacomo, C. Yu.

The text of this book is set in Adobe Garamond.
The illustrations are watercolor and charcoal pencil, reproduced in full color.

Library of Congress Cataloging-in-Publication Data

Curious George goes to a chocolate factory / based on the original character
by Margret and H. A. Rey.
p. cm.
Summary: George's curiosity causes a problem at the chocolate factory, but his quick think-
ing and speedy action on the assembly line help save the candies.
RNF ISBN 0-395-91216-4 PAP ISBN 0-395-91214-8 PABRD ISBN 0-395-92331-X
[1. Chocolate—Fiction. 2. Candy—Fiction. 3. Monkeys—Fiction.] I. Rey, Margret,
1906–1996. II. Rey, H. A. (Hans Augusto), 1898–1977.
PZ7.C92155 1998
[E]—dc21
97-50446
CIP
AC

Manufactured in China

This is George.

George was a good little monkey and always very curious.

One day George went for a drive with his friend, the man with the yellow hat.

"Look, George," the man said. "There's a store in that chocolate factory up ahead. Let's stop for a treat."

George loved chocolates.
Inside the store, boxes of chocolates were stacked everywhere, but the man with the yellow hat found his favorites right away. "George," he said, "wait here while I buy these, and please stay out of trouble."

George looked around the store.
He saw chocolate-covered cherries
and fudge-flavored lollipops.
A chocolate bunny caught his eye.

Then something else caught his eye.
What were all those people looking at?
George was curious.

He climbed up to get
a better look. Through
the window he saw lots
of trays filled with little
brown dots.

What were all those
little brown dots?

George was curious.
He found a door that led
to the other side of the window.

The little brown dots were chocolates, of course! A tour guide was showing a group of people how to tell what was inside the chocolates by looking at the swirls on top.

This little swirl
means fudge,

this one says that
caramel is inside,

and this wiggle is for
marshmallow.

This is the squiggle
for a truffle,

this one is
for nougat,

this sideways swirl is
for orange fluff,

and this one is for George's favorite — banana cream.

George followed the tour group until they came to a balcony
overlooking a room where the chocolates were made. Down below,
busy workers picked the candy off the machines and put them in boxes.

SLOW   MEDIUM   FAST   EXTRA FAST

12

These were the machines that made the chocolates with the swirls on top! The chocolates came out of the machines on long belts. But how did they get their swirls?

George was curious.

He climbed down from the balcony . . .

and up onto a machine.

George peeked inside.
He was trying to see what
was making the swirls when
all of a sudden . . .

the chocolates began
coming out faster and
faster! They sped by him
so quickly they seemed
to be running on legs
of their own.

"Quick! Bring more boxes!" yelled a man with a tall white hat.
"What happened?" asked another man.

Nobody answered. Nobody knew what had happened and everyone was so busy that no one noticed George.

The workers began to fall behind and the candy began to fall off the end of the belt.

"Save the chocolates!" yelled the man with the tall white hat.

Meanwhile, George saw one of his favorites whiz by. He tried to catch the banana-cream chocolate, but it was too fast!

He chased it to the end of the belt.

At the end of the belt a pile of chocolates was growing taller and taller. George had never seen so many chocolates!

As he searched for the banana cream, he put the others in empty boxes.

George was a fast worker. Someone noticed and yelled, "Bring that monkey more boxes! He's helping us catch up!"

Not all the chocolates made it into boxes, but no more chocolates fell on the floor.

Just when George and the workers were all caught up, the tour guide ran in with the man with the yellow hat. "Get that monkey out of here!" she yelled. "He's ruining our chocolates!"

"But this little monkey SAVED the chocolates," explained the workers.

Then the man with the tall white hat said to George, "You may have caused us some trouble, but you were a speedy little monkey. You deserve a big box of candy for all your help."

George was glad he was not in trouble, but he did not take the chocolates.

Back in the parking lot, the workers waved good-bye as George and his friend got into their little blue car.

"George, are you sure you don't want any chocolates before we leave?" asked the man with the yellow hat.

George was sure.